A NEW AMISH LOVE

SARAH MILLER

IRENE GLICK

SWEETBOOKHUB.COM

CHAPTER ONE

FAITH'S CREEK, PENNSYLVANIA.

*T*he flames were red hot, engulfing the house and spreading out so that they singed her skin. Naomi Mast could hear heart wrenching cries, the cries of her husband, David, who was still trapped inside.

"I can't get to you, David. Oh, someone, please, help him," she cried out, cradling their daughter, Hannah in her arms.

She stared desperately up at the flaming inferno, the wooden frame buckling and collapsing in a mass of sparks and fire. The night sky was lit up, the neighbors desperately fetching buckets to douse the flames, which only seemed to grow greater and more ferocious.

"There's nothing we can do," one of them called out, "it's coming down."

In a sudden collapse, the frame toppled. Naomi shrank back, as Hannah began to cry, clutching at Naomi, who could only stare in utter helplessness and desperation at the sight before her.

"Oh, David," she whispered, tears rolling down her cheeks.

"I'm so sorry, Naomi," one of the women said, trying to lead her away.

But Naomi was rooted to the spot, and all she could look at was the burning furnace which only a few hours ago had been her home, the place she was happy, and the place where now her dear husband had met his sorry fate.

Naomi awoke with a start. It was always the same dream. As regular as clockwork, every night. It was torture for her. She went to sleep knowing the inevitability that it would come. The replaying of that terrible night. The night that had changed her life forever.

She breathed a deep sigh, rolling onto her side and peering at the hands of the clock on her bedside table. It was four o'clock in the morning. She was wide awake, and sat up, stretching out her arms and taking a deep breath as she tried to remind herself that it was only a dream, even as it was a reminder of a terrible truth.

The fire had occurred three years previously, its aftermath put behind her. But still, she remembered it as though it were yesterday.

"You're safe, it's over," she told herself, repeating the words she used to try and comfort herself.

It was Bishop Amos Beiler who had suggested that. He had told her she might never move on from her grief, but she could learn to live with it, as hard as it would be.

"Trust in *Gott,*" he had told her, and every night, whenever Naomi awoke from the dreadful dream, she would offer up a silent prayer, not only for herself but for Hannah, too.

She knew her daughter suffered from the same dreams as her. There were nights when Hannah's cries would wake her. These were the worst for she would find her daughter sitting hunched on her bed, shaking with fear at the memory of that dreadful night.

The fire had been an accident, an oil lamp foolishly left burning. Naomi had awoken to the smell of acrid smoke.

Coughing and spluttering she had raced to find Hannah, expecting David to follow her. But in the chaos and confusion, he had become trapped, and outside, Naomi had watched in horror, realizing he was still inside. The neighbors had done their best, but there had been nothing that could save David from his fate, and on that night, Naomi had become a widow at the tender age of twenty-five.

"Coffee time," Naomi told herself.

It was always the same. There was little point in trying to get back to sleep. She would only lie awake for the rest of the night, thinking over everything that had happened. Three years seemed like three minutes, but it also seemed like an eternity. So much had happened in the time since the fire, and yet Naomi could recount every detail, every vivid memory, every moment of that fateful night. She wrapped a night robe around herself and made her way quietly downstairs. Hannah was asleep in the next room, and she did not want to disturb her, knowing how difficult it was for her daughter to sleep the whole night through.

The house was quiet, and Naomi was aware of her footsteps on the stairs, the familiar creak of the fifth step, and the wobble of the banister that her brother-in-law, John Lengacher kept meaning to fix. Naomi lived with her sister, Lily. The fire had cost her everything. She had lost her husband, her home, her security, and everything familiar. She had been left with nothing, and it was only through the kindness of her sister, that she and Hannah had been able to remain in Faith's Creek. Her parents were both dead, and apart from Lily, she had no other family to speak of.

Three years later, Naomi was still living with her sister and trying to forge a new path for herself, one which was proving extremely difficult to find. She lived with her memories and was rarely able to envisage any kind of future for herself. Every day seemed harder than the previous one, and Naomi was rapidly giving up hope of ever escaping from the sad cycle of her living memories and the terrifying nightmares which came with sleep.

"Oh, you startled me," Lily exclaimed, as Naomi entered the kitchen.

The two sisters were the mirror image of one another, with brown hair kept hidden by their prayer *kapps* and bright green eyes. They were as close to twins as sisters could be. But Naomi was the older of the two and had always been the more sensible and thoughtful, even as it was Lily on whom she now relied for everything.

"I didn't think you'd be up. It's just gone four o'clock," Naomi said, staring at her sister in surprise.

"John was snoring, and I thought I heard Hannah stirring. But I've not been sleeping well lately, either. You know how it is when you're carrying. Did you have the dream?" Lily asked.

Naomi nodded. "It's like an inbuilt alarm clock. I can't escape it. Every night, the same dream. Watching the house burn to the ground," she replied, sighing and taking a seat at the kitchen table.

"I'll make you some coffee." Lily smiled and put a match to the stove to boil water.

Lily was pregnant. The *boppli* was due any day. It would mean big changes for them all and Naomi already felt as if she imposed on their happy lives. This was not how it was meant to be. The life that her sister and John lived should have been hers, too. She knew that the arrival of the *boppli* would bring many changes with it, and whilst she was happy for Lily, she knew it would mean a new life for them all. Naomi feared what her own place in that life would be and whether her sister would even want her there in those first throes of maternal bliss.

"I just wish I could stop repeating it over and over again. Every night, the same image, the same terror, the same helplessness," Naomi said, sighing and shaking her head.

"Perhaps you need to speak to Bishop Beiler again. He might be able to help you," Lily replied.

Naomi knew what a burden she placed on her sister. She cooked, she cleaned, she listened, she did everything – not only for Naomi but for Hannah, too. It was not fair, but Naomi could think of no way to make things different. She hated her life, with all its sorrow and worry.

"I'll try," she replied.

Lily made the coffee, and they sat for a while in silence. Naomi could not help but feel terribly guilty for all that had happened. She wanted Lily and John to be happy, but such happiness would only come at her and Hannah's expense, and the thought of such change filled her with dread.

CHAPTER TWO

"*Are* you awake?" Lily whispered as she got back into bed next to John a short while later.

"I am now. It's that creaking stair that always wakes me," John replied, sitting up in bed.

The first rays of light were coming through the curtains, and it would soon be time to get up. Lily had sent Naomi back to bed, promising to see to Hannah when she woke up and imploring her sister to try and get some rest. She was worried about Naomi's recurring dream and desperately wanted to do something to help her.

"I'm worried about Naomi. She keeps waking up with the terrors. It's this dream about the fire. She never gets a peaceful night," Lily said, shaking her head as she sat on the bed next to John.

"You can't stop dreams," he replied.

"*Nee*, but you can't keep having them, either. I don't know what to do. I love her, but... something needs to change if she's ever going to find any peace," Lily said, sighing as she turned to John.

He put his arm around her. "Maybe it's time she stood on her own two feet," he said.

Lily felt her heart stutter and she looked at him curiously. "I don't think it's that simple, John. I think the *boppli's* made her... well, think about the future. I don't know, I can't put my finger on it. But I can't ask her to leave."

She knew John found it difficult sharing their home with Naomi. She did her share of the chores and always offered to help, but the house had always been their own space, and with Naomi and Hannah there, things were sometimes fraught.

"I don't mean that. But the *boppli* is coming... it's going to mean some changes. I've been lying awake tonight, too, and I've got an idea," he said, "one that helps Naomi as well as us."

Lily nodded for him to continue. He was a good man and she was open to suggestions, and she knew she could not just allow things to continue as they had been.

"Well, what is it?" she asked, too wide awake to contemplate going back to sleep.

"It's this..." he began, explaining his idea as Lily listened with interest.

Simeon Whitmer was a baker. He had learned his trade in Philadelphia and had spent a few years living in New York, baking bagels in a Jewish bakery in Brooklyn. But the pace of life in the big city had begun to wear him down, and he had longed for the simpler life of his *kinnerhood*. Simeon was Amish by birth, but he had drifted away from the practice of his faith, only to rediscover it on a chance trip to Pennsylvania. The Greyhound bus had passed close to a place called Faith's Creek, and Simeon had been taken by what he perceived as a simpler way of life.

There was no doubt in his mind that *Gott* had guided him to that moment, and with only a few dollars in his pocket and a prayer in his heart, Simeon had made the move from the city to the country.

He had taken the rent on a small store close to the center of the community and opened it as a bakery, selling everything from bagels and English muffins to apple fritters and cinnamon buns. He made bread every morning, and it had not taken long for word to spread as to the quality of what he produced. Life was busy, and Simeon would rise at four o'clock every morning to start baking and preparing for the day ahead. He lived above the store and had at last found a sense of happiness in life, a life no longer caught up in the hustle and bustle of an anonymous city, but lived amidst a community that had welcomed him with open arms.

"You've certainly put the cat among the pigeons by opening a new bakery," Bishop Amos Beiler had told him.

"And why's that?" Simeon had asked, as he served the Bishop with half a dozen blueberry muffins.

"Well, Faith's Creek already has several bakers; The Miller's, and the newest is Katy Zook. She runs a stall on market days. I'm sure you'll meet her," Amos had replied.

Simeon had not wanted to make an enemy, and he had made it his business to seek out the Millers who were gracious and offered him any help he needed. He then went to Katy Zook and explained himself. He had found her an amicable sort, and the two had agreed that there was room enough in Faith's Creek for them both, particularly considering Katy's specialty – shoofly pie – was a creation Simeon was yet to master.

"I'll teach you how to make it one time," Katy had said, and in return, Simeon had promised to teach her the secret of a baked cheesecake.

Despite having been open for just a few short weeks, Simeon's store was thriving, and he could not have been happier with the move he had made, and the new life in Faith's Creek. Even if there were certain things about his past he would rather forget. He was building up a loyal following, and there was one man, in particular, a blacksmith named John Lengacher, who came in every day.

His order was always the same: an apple fritter and a strong, black coffee. The two men were of a similar age, John having celebrated his thirtieth birthday just a few weeks earlier, and they had soon built up a friendly rapport.

"I don't even need to ask, do I? An apple fritter..." Simeon began.

"And a strong, black coffee," John said, finishing Simeon's sentence with a grin.

"Can't I tempt you with something different? I made blondies this morning, and there's apple strudel, cinnamon turnover, a piece of banana bread?" Simeon said, but John shook his head.

"What can I say? I'm a man of habit. But I'll take two blondies, one for my *fraa* and one for my sister-in-law. They've found out that I come in here every day, and I don't think I'll be welcome at home if I don't take them something back," John replied, smiling at Simeon across the counter.

Simeon had taken an immediate liking to John. He was an affable sort of man, easy to get along with, and always with something interesting to say. He had told Simeon all about Faith's Creek and helped him to settle in at the time he was finding his feet. He had even helped him as he prepared to commit to the church. It was something he had never done, having left on his *rumspringa* and never returned. Simeon was grateful to John, and he counted him as the first true friend he had made in this new beginning.

"Two blondies, an apple fritter, and a strong, black coffee. That'll be $4.50," Simeon said, putting the cakes into a paper bag and pouring the coffee into the cup that John always carried.

"How are you settling in? Are you managing to meet people?" John asked.

Simeon nodded. "I met Katy Zook the other day. Amos thought the two of us might be at odds with the bakery, but we've agreed to keep things professional," he said.

John nodded. "She makes a good shoofly pie, but her bread... it's like rock cakes," he said.

Simeon smiled. "I couldn't possibly comment," he said.

John laughed. "Always the diplomat. Say... I don't know how you're fixed in the evenings. But I wondered if you'd like to come and have dinner with us. We're a bit of a mixed family. There's my *fraa*, Lily, and my sister-in-law, Naomi. She lost her husband a few years back, and she lives with us. And there's my niece, Hannah. She's a sweet little thing. You'd be very welcome any night you're free," he said.

Simeon tended to go to bed early. Apart from John, he was yet to make any real friends in Faith's Creek. It was hard to break into a new community, and he had found it difficult to know how to make friends in a small place after the anonymity of the big city. The irony of living amongst millions of people in New York was that life could be lonely, and Simeon was determined to change that in Faith's Creek.

"I'd like that. I really would," he said.

John smiled. "Tomorrow night? I should probably warn you... Naomi's not in the best way at the moment. She's been struggling ever since David died. It was a house fire three years ago, and she's still not gotten over it. It's hard to know what to do to help her. But I think meeting you would really do her good. She needs company, and something to distract her from all those feelings about the past. I hope you don't think I'm inviting you just for that, but it'll certainly help," he said.

Simeon shook his head. He knew about pain and memories of the past. He was only too pleased to be invited, and he felt a certain sense of curiosity at the prospect of meeting John's sister-in-law.

"It's all right. I understand. We've all got a past. But it's the future that matters, isn't it? I'll be pleased to meet Naomi. And didn't you say the other day your *fraa's* pregnant?" Simeon asked, recalling a conversation he and John had shared the week before.

"That's right. Between you and me, I think the thought of the *boppli* coming is what's causing Naomi to feel unsettled. She'll be all right, but I'm glad you're coming to meet her. I think it'll really help," he said, taking his bag of cakes and cup of coffee off the counter.

"All right, well, I'll see you tomorrow for your apple fritter and then in the evening for dinner," Simeon said, and he wished John goodbye, smiling to himself at the thought of meeting new people and sharing dinner with John and his family.

As the store door closed, Simeon pulled out a handkerchief from his pocket. It was white with blue trim. He always carried one of the set – seven in total, one for every day of the week. It was his connection to the past, a way of remembering what had been, even as he looked to the future. The handkerchief was embroidered with his initials, and he thought back to the day it had been stitched by the first woman he had ever loved. But the memory was painful – as much as he wanted to experience it – and he placed the handkerchief quickly back into his pocket.

"A new start, Simeon," he told himself, repeating the words he had often spoken as he planned his move to Faith's Creek.

CHAPTER THREE

"*T*hat's very nice, Hannah. You're such a good drawer. Maybe you'll grow up to be an artist," Naomi said, peering over Hannah's shoulder as she sat at the kitchen table.

Hannah was four years old, but there was no denying her obvious talent for art. She loved to draw, and the house was littered with her pictures and paintings, stuck up all around. Naomi was pleased to encourage this fledgling talent. It was a way of distracting Hannah from her troubles, and it helped Naomi, too. Being Hannah's *mamm* was the one thing that kept her going. She had to be strong for her daughter's sake, and taking care of Hannah was her reason for getting up in the morning.

"I drew you," Hannah said, looking up at Naomi.

"And it's very good."

"I drew you smiling, so you'd be happy," she said.

Naomi felt the tears rising in her eyes. "That's very sweet of you, Hannah. I'm glad you want your *mamm* to smile and be happy," she said.

The picture was very pretty. It showed Naomi standing in front of the house, surrounded by flowers and with a big smile on her face. It was not how Naomi felt, but it was how she wanted to feel, if only for Hannah's sake. She wanted to put the past behind her, but her memories held her back.

"I wanted to draw *daed*, but I don't know what he looks like," Hannah said, and now Naomi could not hold back the tears. They rolled down her cheek and dropped onto the picture.

"Oh... well, he was very tall and had hair just like yours – blonde with streaks of brown. He always smiled, so you could draw him smiling, and he had bright blue eyes. We could draw him together next time you want to do a picture," she said.

Hannah nodded. "I'd like that," she said, as Lily entered the room.

"Oh, look at this. Aren't you clever?" Lily said as Naomi held out the picture.

"I'll draw one of you, too, Aunt Lily," Hannah said, but Naomi shook her head.

"Not now, though. Aunt Lily's busy preparing for tonight," she said, glancing at her sister, who smiled.

Naomi was not looking forward to the evening. Her sister and brother-in-law had invited a man named Simeon Whitmer for dinner. He was the owner of a new bakery in Faith's Creek, and John had befriended him over the past few weeks. Apparently, he made the most delicious apple fritters John had ever tasted, and having tried several of the cakes John had brought home, Naomi was in no doubt as to the baker's skills. But as for meeting him in person, Naomi was less convinced.

She knew what John was trying to do. Ever since the fire, well-meaning individuals in Faith's Creek had suggested she would be happier if she found another husband. But they did not think about how she felt in the present. In their eyes, a husband was the solution to all her troubles, and the memory of David was of no account.

Marriage was not something she desired, not when she still lived with the horror of that dreadful night. She was still in love with David and had as much respect for her wedding vows in widowhood as she had in marriage. John and Lily were only trying to help, she knew that, but still, she would have preferred a quiet evening with Hannah, rather than one involving small talk with a stranger.

"Will you come and help me peel the potatoes?" Lily asked as Hannah got down from the table.

"Then we'll get you settled for bed," Naomi said, glancing at the clock on the wall, which said six o'clock.

Simeon was due in an hour, and there was still plenty to do. The table needed setting, the last of the dishes needed washing, and the apple pie which Lily had made was still not baked.

"I'm worried he won't like it. It's nerve-wracking baking for a baker," Lily said, as she put the pie in the oven.

"I'm sure he's just pleased to be invited over for dinner. You heard what John said. He doesn't know anyone in Faith's Creek yet, not properly," Naomi replied.

"He sounds like a nice person. He's been living in New York and before that, Philadelphia. I don't know why he'd move to a place like this," Lily said.

Naomi laughed. "It isn't that bad," she said.

The two of them had grown up in Faith's Creek. It was the only home Naomi had ever known. Their parents had owned a small holding and their *daed* had mended buggies. Life was simple, but Naomi could think of nowhere else she would rather be. Faith's Creek was her solace, as well as a place filled with unhappy memories. There were times she had thought about leaving, but in truth, there was nowhere else she would rather be.

"I don't mean it like that. But after the hustle and bustle of the city, it seems strange for a man to uproot himself and move to a small place like this. I love Faith's Creek, but it's not exactly Times Square, is it?" Lily replied, turning her attention to the potatoes that Hannah had been tasked with scrubbing.

"Maybe he just wanted a change. It's not so strange, is it?" Naomi replied, even as she thought again about her own clinging to the past.

Change was not something that came naturally to Naomi. She did not want to change. She lived in the past and was scared of the possibility of something new detracting from what she clung to – the memories of David.

"Well, I'll be glad to meet him. He sounds like a decent sort of man. It'll be good for you to meet him, too," she said, and Naomi rolled her eyes.

"Is this some kind of matchmaking attempt?" she asked, fixing her sister with a hard stare.

This was what Naomi feared. She knew Lily and John meant well. Lily often spoke of her desire to see Naomi happy, but this was the first time either of them had done something practical to further their ends. Naomi did not like being "set up" like this. If she wanted to meet a man, she would meet him in her own way, rather than around the dinner table.

A sigh escaped her. She had nothing to say to him. Her life revolved around Hannah and her job taking in mending and ironing for a dozen or so families who lived nearby. Nothing was exciting or interesting about her, or so she believed. Naomi had never traveled far from Faith's Creek; she had not even had a *rumspringa*. Her life had been devastated at the moment it was supposed to blossom. Tragedy was her only reference point, and that was hardly the beginning of a conversation.

"No... but... it wouldn't do you any harm to meet someone new, would it? He's a nice man, by all accounts, and John thinks he's got a past of sorts. We don't know the details, but he must have had a reason to leave the city. Just talk to him. Maybe you'll surprise yourself," Lily said.

Naomi sighed.

What choice did she have but to agree? She would be polite and join in the conversation. But she knew her mind would be elsewhere. She was already thinking about the night ahead, worrying about the inevitability of recounting her memories in her dreams. The thought of it preoccupied her, and, as the appointed hour approached, Naomi knew that however charming Simeon Whitmer might be, her thoughts would remain with another man.

CHAPTER FOUR

*S*imeon was nervous. This was the first time he had been invited to dinner by anyone in a long time. In New York, he had had acquaintances, people to pass the time of day with, but not to socialize with. He had often found himself lost in the busyness of everyday life, unable to step out of the rat race and embrace something new.

That was one of the reasons he had come to Faith's Creek, and he was glad to have had the opportunity of meeting new people and realizing that a different way of life was possible. John had kindly come to fetch him in the family's buggy and the two of them were riding along together, approaching the house that his friend shared with his wife, sister-in-law, and niece.

"We planted an orchard twenty years ago when I was a boy. We're reaping the rewards now. We had such a good crop last year. It all went to juice, though Lily was making apple pies with the windfalls for three months. It's apple pie tonight. I hope you like it," John said, as they passed the orchard, where the trees were budding with fruit.

"It's a great place. Do you farm it all yourself?" John asked, looking around the plot with interest.

The house lay at the center of a small holding. There was the orchard, along with a large vegetable field and flower borders. The garden at the front of the house was laid to lawn, and a little girl, perhaps four years old, was playing there. Simeon smiled at the sight. He liked *kinner* and always seemed to get on well with them.

As they approached, she looked up and smiled. John reined the buggy in, waving to the little girl, who came to greet them.

"Isn't it about your bedtime, Hannah?" John asked, as the two men climbed down from the buggy.

"*Mamm* said I could play outside until bedtime," the little girl replied.

"This is Simeon, Hannah, he's coming for dinner. And Simeon, this is Hannah, my niece," John said, smiling as Simeon held out his hand.

"It's a pleasure to meet you. It looks like you've been busy there," he said, pointing to a daisy chain that Hannah was weaving.

"It's for my *mamm*. I want her to look pretty, just like she does in my pictures," Hannah replied.

"Hannah's very good at art. You'll see her pictures all around the house," John said.

"Is that so? Shall I help you finish this?" Simeon said, settling himself down on the grass.

It was a warm evening, the sun was still sitting lazily above the horizon, and Simeon was happy being outside, with the enticing scent of dinner wafting from an open window nearby.

"It's nearly done. You can thread this one, though," Hannah said, handing Simeon a daisy.

She was a sweet little thing, and Simeon could not help but feel sorry for her at the thought of her having lost her *daed*. John had explained a little more of the family history during their buggy ride, and Simeon knew what a tragedy it was that had claimed the life of David Mast. The thought of it was too terrible to comprehend, even as Simeon shuddered at the thought of just how easy the perfect life could be ripped away.

Hannah had just finished her daisy garland when the door to the house opened, and a woman appeared. She had a smile on her face and a lock of brown hair had escaped her *kapp*.

"Aren't you coming in, John? Or were you just going to keep our guest outside all evening?" she asked.

"We got talking to Hannah, but we'll come in, now," John said, as Simeon rose to his feet and dusted himself off.

"I'm sorry, I'm being terribly rude," he said, hurrying to greet the woman, who now introduced herself as Lily, John's wife.

"Not at all. We're glad to have you here. I hope you're hungry. There's no shortage of food," she said, ushering him up the porch steps.

Despite being a baker, Simeon found little time to cook for himself. Meals were snatched, and the opportunity for decent, home-cooked food was limited. He had been looking forward to the meal, and John had told him what an excellent cook his wife was.

"It's very kind of you to invite me. I'm so glad I came to Faith's Creek. It's such a lovely place, and the people are so welcoming," he said, following Lily inside.

The house was cozy and comfortable. The parlor was well-furnished, and the walls were covered in Hannah's pictures. A large dining table, set for four, stood in the corner, and a door stood open, leading to the kitchen, from which the most delicious smells were emanating.

"Won't you sit down?" John said, pointing to a chair by the stove.

"I'll get you a glass of apple juice. It's ours from last year's harvest. It's delicious," Lily said.

Simeon already felt right at home, and he sat down, admiring the pictures, as Hannah came to sit on the rug by the stove. She was still holding the daisy chain in her hand, and she smiled at Simeon, tilting her head to one side and watching him.

"You're a real artist, Hannah. They're very good," he said, smiling back at her.

"I like to draw pictures of my *mamm*," she said, and Simeon now realized most of the pictures showed a tall, attractive woman with long brown hair beneath her *kapp* and bright green eyes.

They were drawn with the naivety of a *kinner's* hand, but there was no mistaking the obvious talent.

"You've chosen a good subject, Hannah," he said, just as Lily returned from the kitchen with a glass of apple juice for him.

"I hope you like it," she said, smiling at him.

"I was just saying to Hannah, she's chosen a good subject for her drawings," Simeon replied, glancing around the room.

"She loves drawing. She's always been good at it. It helps her, I think. She didn't know her *daed*, but she still feels his loss. Now, won't you come and sit at the table?" she asked, and Simeon nodded.

His stomach was rumbling, and he came to join John at the table, where half a dozen dishes had been laid out for them to enjoy. There were buttered noodles, a chicken pie, beef croquettes, mashed potatoes, a dish of greens, and another of carrots. There was a fresh loaf of bread, too, with a large pat of butter, and two jugs, one containing apple juice and another water with wedges of lemon in it. It was a veritable feast, and Simeon was urged to sit down and help himself. The table had been neatly laid and there were freshly laundered napkins at every setting. John and Lily sat down, too, so that only one space remained.

"Hannah, will you go up and tell your *mamm* we're ready to eat. She'll put you to bed quickly," Lily said.

Hannah nodded.

"Goodnight, Lily. I'm pleased to have met you," Simeon said, smiling at Hannah, who sighed.

"I want to give *mamm* the flower garland," Hannah said, looking up at Lily with wide, imploring eyes.

"Can't she stay up this one time?" John asked, and Lily relented.

"All right, but go and call your *mamm*. We're ready to say grace and eat," Lily said.

Simeon watched as Hannah made her way to the stairs, calling out for her *mamm* as she went. Lily looked embarrassed.

"I'm sorry about Naomi. She's... well, she's not used to having people here, that's all. It's not been easy for her recently," she said, glancing nervously at John.

"It's all right. I understand. It's not always easy meeting new people," he said.

"But you've done pretty well at it. It's a big thing moving from the city to a place like this. What made you choose Faith's Creek?" John asked, helping himself to mashed potatoes.

"It was quite by chance, really. I was on my way to Pittsburgh and the Greyhound bus came through here. There was something about Faith's Creek that caught my eye. I was raised Amish, as you know, but it never really stuck. Still, I don't think you ever lose that... grounding, if that's what you'd call it. I was ready for a change and where better than a place like this after the pace of life in New York?" he said, helping himself from the dish of carrots.

"Well. We're glad you came here, even if our waistlines aren't! The whole community's talking about your baking," John said, smiling across the table.

"I can't help it if people eat too much. It's good for business," Simeon said, laughing, just as a footfall on the stairs caused him to look up.

A woman was standing there, a woman who could only be the same one depicted on the walls all around the parlor. She was looking shyly at them, and with a nervous smile on her face.

"Oh, there you are. Come and have some dinner and meet Simeon. We're just talking about our waistlines now he's opened yet another bakery in Faith's Creek," Lily said.

Simeon smiled at Naomi. She was a very pretty woman, striking, in fact. He rose to his feet to greet her, but she nodded briefly and then averted her gaze, coming to sit down at the table, as Hannah sat down on the rug.

"She liked her flower chain," Hannah said.

"I'm glad. Won't you help yourself, Simeon? There's plenty to go around," she said, but Simeon was hardly listening.

He could not take his eyes off Naomi, even as she averted her gaze from him. He thought she was beautiful. It was the strangest feeling, one he had to check in order not to appear rude.

"Oh... thank you," he replied, reaching out for the bowl of buttered noodles, still with one eye on Naomi, who was sitting opposite him with her head bowed.

CHAPTER FIVE

*N*aomi was fed up. She had done her best to be polite and make small-talk. It was not that she disliked Simeon, but the whole premise of the dinner – an attempt at matchmaking – was hardly something she relished. Lily had made an effort with the food. It was delicious, and Hannah had joined them at the table, allowed to try a little of everything. Naomi was wearing the garland of flowers that Hannah had made for her. It was a sweet gesture and a reminder to Naomi of just how lucky she was to have a daughter like Hannah.

"I really think the bakery could go from strength to strength. Back in New York, I used to make wedding cakes, and I know weddings here sometimes have two or three cakes to feed all the guests. I decorate them, too," Simeon was saying.

"Oh, you'll be very popular, then. It's not easy to find someone to make a decent wedding cake. Do you remember ours, John? It was lopsided," Lily said, shaking her head and laughing.

"It didn't taste too bad, though. We've still got a piece of it somewhere, I think," John said, smiling at Simeon who laughed.

"Hopefully, I'll get them right. But it's just one way I think I could make the business thrive. Eventually, I'd like to employ someone else to help. It's an early start every morning to get the dough mixed and onto prove," he said.

"I've got a wonderful recipe for a no knead bread. All you do is mix it up the night before, like put it in a Dutch oven to bake. It's foolproof," Lily said.

Naomi was listening to the conversation, but she had only said two words all night. She wanted to go to bed. She had been awake since four o'clock that morning, and she was starting to feel tired, even though she knew the grim prospect that her dreams would bring.

"What about you, Naomi? What was your wedding cake like?" Simeon asked.

Naomi looked up in surprise.

He was not to know how much she disliked talking about the past, even as it preoccupied her thoughts. Even the happy memories such as her wedding day or the birth of Hannah were tinged with sadness at the loss of what might have been. She tensed up, glancing at Lily, who looked suddenly worried.

"Oh, we don't normally..." Lily began, but Naomi interrupted her.

"It was nice," she said, not wishing to embarrass their guest, but wanting to put an immediate halt on the conversation for the sake of her own feelings.

"I'm glad," Simeon said.

"You're not wearing your garland," Hannah said.

Naomi was grateful to Hannah for the interruption. For a moment she had felt as if the earth was not steady as if she was being pulled into the past.

Naomi had taken the woven daisy chain off to eat, but Hannah now picked it up from the table and placed it over Naomi's head.

"There now. Does it look all right?" Naomi asked, and her daughter nodded.

"You look like a princess," she said.

Naomi couldn't help but smile. "I'm glad you think so," she said, putting her hand on Hannah's cheek and smiling at her.

She looked so like her *daed*, so like David. It brought a tear to Naomi's eye, and she had to turn away, anxious not to let her emotions get the better of her.

"Simeon helped me make it," Hannah said.

Naomi looked up and caught their guest's eye.

He looked embarrassed and began to protest.

"I only threaded a few flowers, Hannah. It was kind of you to let me help you," he said, turning red.

"That's very kind of you, isn't it, Hannah?" Naomi replied.

She knew she had been rude in sitting back from the conversation. Simeon was clearly a good man, with a kind heart. Hannah had a way of reading people. She was a trusting little girl, and her instincts were usually right. Naomi could not help but be grateful to Simeon for his natural kindness towards her daughter, and, in that moment, she resolved to make more of an effort as Lily announced dessert.

"It's an apple pie. I hope it's all right," she said, glancing nervously at Simeon.

"I'm sure it'll be delicious. It might surprise you to know that when I was learning to make apple pie, I burned two dozen before I made one that was edible," he said, shaking his head and laughing.

There was something genuine about him. He was open and honest, qualities which Naomi admired. She liked him, even as she did not like Lily and John's attempts at matchmaking. Naomi had always vowed to remain loyal to David, and she took that loyalty seriously.

"And some cream, too," Lily said, handing a bowl and jug to Simeon, who smiled.

"That's quite a slab of pie," he said, glancing at Naomi, who tried hard not to laugh.

The conversation now proceeded in a livelier tone, and Naomi forced herself to join in, interested in learning more about their guest.

"What was it like living in those big cities? I've been to Philadelphia, but New York must seem like a whole other place," John said after they had finished their dessert.

"It's a remarkable place, I'll admit it. You can be anything you want to be there, and there's every permutation of life. It's overwhelming at times. I think that's why every neighborhood has its own feel, its own identity. People like to think they belong, even in a metropolis. But I'm glad I've swapped it for this. Faith's Creek might not have a Guggenheim or an Empire State Building, but it's got a soul, and I like that," he replied.

"Then you'll never go back?" Naomi asked.

"He's only just got here," her sister said, tutting.

"I don't think so. I left a lot behind, but I'm pleased to be looking ahead to the future," he replied.

He did not elaborate further on what he had left behind, but Naomi could tell he was carrying something in his heart, a memory he kept buried. She knew it because it was the same look she had, too, that same clinging to the past, the same look she saw every day in the mirror. Simeon was a kindred spirit, or so she thought. But whilst he had run from his memories, Naomi remained in the very place they had been forged.

CHAPTER SIX

"Well, we've had a lovely evening. You're welcome here anytime. In fact, I insist on it," Lily said, as they bid Simeon goodbye.

"I only wish I could repay the hospitality, but the bedsit over the bakery isn't exactly the best place to host a dinner party," Simeon replied, pulling on his boots.

"You've more than repaid it in apple fritters and cinnamon buns," John replied, offering his hand to Simeon.

Hannah was fast asleep on the rug in front of the stove, and Naomi lifted her up, whispering in her ear.

"Are you going to say goodbye to Simeon?" she asked.

"Goodbye," Hannah replied, sleepily opening her eyes.

"I'll take her upstairs," Lily said, and before Naomi could protest, she had taken Hannah from her arms and was making her way towards the stairs, calling out a final farewell to Simeon, as John opened the door.

"Well, goodnight," Simeon said, smiling at Naomi.

"I'll... step out with you. It's still a lovely evening," Naomi said, suddenly struck by a desire to speak with Simeon alone.

She did not know what prompted such a feeling, only that it felt right to follow it through. John closed the door behind them, and the two of them were left on the porch, looking out over the small-holding. The sun was only just beginning to set, and there was a pleasant scent in the air, the sweet smell of flowers and cut grass.

"It's been such a nice evening. I'm really pleased to meet you. You're so lucky with Hannah, she's a real credit to you," Simeon said, as they stepped down onto the path leading through the garden.

"She brings out the best in me," Naomi replied.

She was still wearing the garland which Hannah had made for her, and now Simeon stooped down and picked some of the dandelions growing in the grass. She watched as he split the ends open, weaving the flowers into a bracelet that he offered her.

"To go with the garland," he said.

Naomi blushed. It felt wrong to accept such a gift, even though it was meant in kindness. She thought of David and her vows, and she shook her head.

"Oh, you're very kind, but I couldn't," she said, and he looked at her in surprise.

"I'm sorry. Did I offend you?" he asked.

"No... it's not that, it's just..." she replied, her words trailing off.

It was only a bracelet made of flowers, but it seemed to represent far more. She felt torn between accepting the gesture and honoring her memories. Why had she even stepped out of the house as Simeon left? It was all so confusing.

"I'm sorry if I overstepped the mark," he said.

Naomi shook her head.

She did not want to upset him. He was only being kind, and she felt terrible for making him think he had done something wrong.

"You didn't. It's just... I'm still grieving for my husband," she said.

He nodded. "I understand," he replied, and there was something about the tone of his voice which made Naomi believe he really did understand her.

"Don't think I'm not flattered," she said, sensing his feelings.

"I'm just pleased to meet you, that's all. I got carried away... but say... would you and Hannah like to come by the bakery one time? I'm trying to perfect a new recipe, it's for honey bread. Perhaps she'd like to see how it's made," he said, blushing and turning away his gaze.

Naomi was not about to refuse another kind gesture, especially one directed at Hannah, too. She smiled and nodded.

"I'd like that, and I know Hannah would, too," she replied, and Simeon looked up with a grin on his face.

"That's great. Well, come by anytime. Tomorrow, if you like," he said.

Naomi nodded. "We'll come," she said, and for a moment, their eyes met in a lingering gaze.

There was such kindness in his eyes, and Naomi could not help but be attracted to him, even as she tried to resist such feelings, too.

"Great, well, I'll see you both soon," he replied, and nodding to her, he hurried off along the path and out of the gate, turning to wave to her from the path leading back to Faith's Creek.

Naomi watched him go. She sighed, glancing down at the garland of flowers around her neck, and once again feeling guilty for rejecting the gift of the bracelet. Simeon was a good man – she could tell that from just an evening spent in his company. But she wondered, too, what burden it was he was carrying, and what memories he held of the past. She returned inside, finding Lily clearing the last of the dishes from the table.

"I've put her to bed. She couldn't stop talking about Simeon," Lily said, smiling as Naomi sat down at the table.

"He certainly seems a good man," Naomi replied.

"There's no doubt about that. I'm glad the two of you met. There's no harm in it, Naomi. You deserve to be happy," Lily said.

Naomi thought about these words. Her sister was right, of course. She *did* deserve to be happy, but allowing herself to be was another matter. She felt held back by the past, and unable to let go of those things which prevented her from looking to the future. But here was an opportunity for something different, and Naomi knew if she did not embrace the moment, she might forever live in the past.

CHAPTER SEVEN

*I*t was 4 o'clock in the morning and still dark. Simeon was barely awake, fumbling his way around the bedsit above the bakery. He splashed water on his face and yawned, looking at himself in the mirror above the sink, illuminated in the light of a lamp hanging nearby.

"Come on, liven up, those loaves won't bake themselves," he said out loud, rubbing his eyes and straightening himself up.

He stretched out his arms, yawning again, before smiling at the memory of the previous evening. He had enjoyed the dinner with Lily and John, and he had enjoyed meeting Naomi and Hannah, too. She was a delightful woman, and his thoughts lingered on her as he made his way downstairs. By now, his routine was well practiced, and he lit the ovens before mixing the first batch of dough. It was a cake day, too, and he soon had half a dozen bowls filled with flour, sugar, and butter, to which he would add different flavorings to make the vast array of cakes he prided himself on offering. But despite his busyness, Simeon could not get the thought of Naomi out of his mind.

"You know she's not interested," he told himself, thinking back to the awkward moment when he had handed her the bracelet made of flowers.

It had been meant as a mere gesture, but he realized now what it had meant to her. The loss of her husband was still an open wound, one which Simeon knew might never heal. He had sensed a sadness in her, a sadness that ran deep. The bracelet had meant more than just a simple token of an evening spent together, and Simeon knew he had to be cautious in the way he approached their fledgling friendship. His invitation to the bakery had been spontaneous, and he was glad Naomi had accepted. He was looking forward to seeing her again – and Hannah – to that end the bowl containing the ingredients for the honey bread now stood on one side, waiting to be mixed.

* * *

"Does she look all right?" Naomi asked, standing Hannah in front of Lily, who smiled and nodded.

"She looks very pretty with ribbons in her hair. And so do you, Naomi," she replied.

Naomi blushed. She was wearing her *kapp*, a blue shawl, and was wearing a new dress in blue check. She and Hannah were about to leave for the bakery, and whilst Naomi felt nervous, she knew that doing so was a step in the right direction. She and Hannah had to stand on their own two feet, and she could not hope to always rely on Lily and John for all her needs – be that material or emotional. Naomi had thought a lot about Simeon since the night before and she had come to the conclusion that there was no harm in making friends, especially a friend who had taken so readily to Hannah.

"I don't need to look pretty, but... *denke*. You'll be all right, won't you?" Naomi asked, for Lily had been suffering from morning sickness that day and was looking rather pale.

"I'll be fine. Just bring me back a cinnamon swirl. I think I'm getting cravings," she replied.

It was a bright, sunny day. John was working on the smallholding, and he waved to Naomi and Hannah as they went by.

"Bring me back an apple fritter," he called out, grinning as Naomi rolled her eyes.

"It's useful having a baker as a friend, isn't it?" she replied.

She took Hannah's hand, feeling quite amazed at herself for what she was doing. It was rare for her to leave the house for the sole purpose of enjoying herself. But the invitation from Simeon had been a kind one, and when she had told Hannah about it that morning, her daughter had been thrilled.

"Will I really get to mix the bread, *mamm?*" Hannah asked.

"Simeon's going to teach us how to make it. That's what he said," she replied.

Hannah's face lit up and she leaped up and down with excitement.

The market was busy that morning, and there was a queue outside the bakery. Naomi could see Simeon serving behind the counter, and she and Hannah waited outside until the last of the customers had emerged with their bread and cakes.

"You're certainly doing a roaring trade," Naomi said, as she led Hannah into the shop.

"I'm all sold out. I don't know what it is, but the whole of Faith's Creek wants bread this morning. Anyway, I'll close up now, then we'll go through to the back. I saved you both an apple fritter," he said, pointing to two cakes on the counter at the back of the store.

Naomi smiled, and Hannah's eyes lit up.

"Can I, *Mamm?*" she asked, and Naomi nodded.

"Just don't tell Aunt Lily – you'll spoil your dinner," she said.

Simeon closed the store and led them through a door at the back and into a small kitchen where enormous sacks of flour and bags of sugar stood on a table in the center. It seemed astonishing to think he could produce so much in such a small space, and he smiled at them, holding out his hand as though showing off a prized possession.

"Here's where it all happens," he said.

"You make everything in here? It's so small," Naomi replied.

"You'd be surprised what you can do in a small space. Here, I'll show you," he said, and he led them over to where a large metal bowl was covered with a cloth.

"Is that honey bread?" Hannah asked.

"Not quite yet, but I'll show you how I make it. Now, I need some butter..." Simeon said, but at that moment, there came a knock at the bakery door.

"You'd better get that," Naomi said, as Simeon looked torn between politeness and the prospect of a customer.

"I'll only be a moment," he said, disappearing out of the kitchen.

"What's this for?" Hannah asked, pointing to a large tin with round holes in it.

"I think it's for muffins," Naomi replied, just as Simeon returned to the kitchen, followed by Sarah Beiler.

The Bishop's *fraa* smiled to see Naomi and Hannah standing by the counter. Naomi had always liked Sarah. She had been so kind to her after David had died, and had often taken care of Hannah when Naomi had needed time on her own to grieve.

"Well, now. This is a lovely surprise, isn't it?" she said, smiling at them both.

Hannah ran over to greet her.

"Simeon's showing us how to make honey bread," Hannah said.

"Is he, now? That's lovely. I'd like to see that, too," Sarah replied.

Simeon was only too happy to show them. Sarah had come to the store in the hope of buying some apple fritters – Bishop Beiler's favorite. But she assured Simeon that a slice of honey bread would go down very well, too, and the loaf was soon in the oven, its aroma filling the air.

"It's really quite easy when you know how," Simeon said, closing the oven door.

"It was kind of you to invite Naomi and Hannah to see it. Why don't I take Hannah out to see the horse? I came in the buggy as I've got some errands to run," Sarah said.

It was as though she had sensed the need to leave Naomi and Simeon alone. Naomi's heart was beating fast, but she could hardly refuse the offer, especially when Hannah gave an excited exclamation and begged to be allowed to see Sarah's horse.

"All right, but only for a moment," Naomi said, and Sarah took Hannah by the hand and led her out of the kitchen.

Naomi and Simeon were left alone, and he smiled at her, glancing at the oven and checking the clock.

"It'll take about twenty minutes to bake," he said.

"It already smells delicious. I can't wait to try some," Naomi replied.

"I just wanted to say... I'm sorry again about last night. About the bracelet, I mean. I was only trying to be friendly," Simeon said.

Naomi blushed. "Oh, think nothing of it. It was sweet of you. It's just... oh, I don't know. I find those sorts of gestures hard," she said, not really knowing how to respond.

There was no doubt in Naomi's mind as to Simeon's kindness, but it was a kindness she found difficult to accept.

"I understand. I think the two of us might have more in common than you think. It's not easy, is it? Memories, I mean," he said.

Naomi nodded. Had he lost someone too?

She felt relaxed in his company. It was a strange sensation, one she rarely experienced. Hannah, Lily, and John were her world, and apart from church on a Sunday, she rarely ventured beyond the confines of the emotional circle she had made for herself. This was a risk, a moment of vulnerability, but she had the feeling she could trust him. The arrival of Sarah Beiler had seemed like a sign, a prompt for Naomi to lower her barriers and invite a friendship she sorely needed.

"Not at all. It's just... I'm not used to this. I'm not very good at making friends or meeting new people. I've kept myself so closed off in the past few years. It feels strange to meet someone new. I know it sounds foolish. John was only trying to help," she said, realizing she was stammering her words, and feeling suddenly embarrassed at the thought of making a fool of herself.

"John was keen for me to meet you. I don't know anyone in Faith's Creek apart from him. I was glad of the dinner invitation. It was kind of him. And I'm glad we met, too. I don't mean anything by that. I'm not trying to make you feel uncomfortable," he said.

"You're just being nice. I'm not used to it. I've avoided people being nice to me for so long. It's strange to just have a normal conversation with someone," she replied.

It was strange, but it was nice, too. She liked him, and she felt comfortable letting down her guard.

"It's the same for me. I told you what life was like in New York. It was hard to meet anyone new. I kept myself to myself for so long. I know you must miss your husband terribly, but I'm sure he'd not want you to keep yourself shut away forever. For Hannah's sake, too," he said.

He was right, of course. Naomi could not live her whole life shut up in the house. The arrival of Lily's baby was about to bring with it a change for them all. She could not live her life as a recluse, and Hannah deserved better.

"He was a good man. He worked hard for us, and he supported us. I thought we'd be together until our old age. But it wasn't meant to be. I still don't understand why he was taken so young and so terribly. I'm sorry, I'm not used to talking like this," Naomi said, feeling the tears welling up in her eyes.

"Don't worry. I understand. But there's no harm in letting yourself live a little. We can be friends, can't we?" he said, and Naomi nodded.

"I'd like that," she replied, and he smiled, reaching out to take her hand in his.

Naomi's heart was beating even faster now. No man had touched her like that since David. A shiver ran through her, not of fear, but of trepidation. Could she allow herself this moment of unexpected happiness? She wondered if this could be the beginning of something new – for her and for Hannah. She smiled at him, holding his gaze, and took a deep breath.

"Shall we see if the honey bread's ready?" Simeon asked.

"I think it is," she said, still smiling at him, their hands joined and an unspoken bond formed between them.

CHAPTER EIGHT

When Naomi left the bakery that afternoon, it felt as though something had changed.

Something *had* changed.

She had allowed herself something so long denied: a moment of happiness.

In Simeon's company, Naomi had felt as though she was a different person than the shadow she had become. Life had seemed so empty and meaningless – save for Hannah – in the years following David's death. Naomi had been existing, not living. But in Simeon's company, she had caught a glimpse of what once had been, a glimpse which had brought her to imagine a brighter future.

Simeon had cut the loaf of honey bread in half, giving Hannah the bigger piece to take home, but it had been the question he had asked Naomi which had been the greater gift.

"Would you like to meet tomorrow? I close the bakery for a half day on Tuesdays. Perhaps we could take Hannah for a picnic by the creek," he had said.

Naomi had been taken aback by his kindness, and she had agreed immediately, marveling at the sense of freedom that such a decision gave her. She had always imagined she would feel guilt at accepting the advances of another man, but in Simeon, she found a man she was certain David would approve of.

"You're just getting to know him," she told herself, as she and Hannah walked home later that afternoon.

But Naomi was only too happy to get to know Simeon, and that happiness was evident on her face when Lily met them at the door.

Lily smiled, raising an eyebrow.

Naomi nodded, yes she had enjoyed herself and didn't mind her sister knowing.

With a big smile, Lily turned to Hannah. "Did you watch the honey bread being made?" she asked.

Hannah nodded, holding up the cloth-wrapped loaf. "We brought some for you," she said.

"We'll all need to go on a diet soon," Lily replied, glancing at Naomi, who laughed.

"It was really kind of Simeon to show us around the bakery," she said, as Hannah ran into the house to find her uncle and show him what she had made.

"It's obviously done you the world of good," Lily said.

Naomi looked at her curiously. "What do you mean?" she asked.

"You're smiling, Naomi. I haven't seen you smile like that since... well, since David was alive," Lily replied.

"I feel like smiling," Naomi said, and that was the honest truth. Maybe she could be happy again?

The next day, Naomi and Hannah set off to meet Simeon by the creek. He had promised to bring a picnic for them all and was waiting for them at the spot they had arranged to meet. It was where a path ran down to the water's edge.

"I'm glad I found it all right. I thought I might get lost. It's beautiful down here," he said, smiling at Naomi as Hannah ran forward to greet him.

Once again, Naomi was surprised by just how quickly Hannah had taken to Simeon. She could be shy at times, but there was no doubt Simeon had a spark about him, one which could not fail to draw others to him – Naomi included.

"I love walking by the creek. I find it such a peaceful place," Naomi said, smiling at him as Hannah ran ahead of them.

He was carrying a large wicker basket and was dressed in an open white shirt and breeches. He looked very handsome, and Naomi could not help but feel at ease in his company. They had known one another just a few short days, but there seemed to be an understanding between them, one which Naomi felt was blossoming like the pretty flowers which grew along the banks of the creek.

"I think it's going to become a favorite place for me, too. And Hannah certainly seems to like it," Simeon said, as Hannah now turned and urged them to walk faster.

"I can see the water," she called out.

They made their way towards a small pool, where a large willow tree provided dappled shade against the sun. It was a warm day, and Simeon opened the basket to reveal chilled bottles of lemonade and cherryade, along with enough food to feed a family of ten.

"I hope I've not brought too much," he said, grinning at her.

"Did you make all this yourself?" she asked, marveling at the sight of the sandwiches, pastries, and cakes he now produced.

"Try the bagels. I learned to make them in New York at the Jewish bakery I worked at. It's not easy to make a good bagel," he said, passing her a box containing half a dozen of the freshly baked bagels.

"It all looks delicious," she said, helping herself to one, as Hannah ran off to play by the water's edge.

"Stay where we can see you, Hannah," Simeon called out, and Naomi smiled.

"You're certainly good with *kinner*," she said.

Simeon lowered his head, but not in time to hide the blush that colored his cheeks.

"I've always wanted *kinner*. I like their company. They make me feel... young, I suppose," he said, helping himself to a pretzel.

Did she see sadness in him, was there a secret in his past?

CHAPTER NINE

"You never married?" Naomi asked, worrying a little that she was pushing him too much.

There was so much she did not know about him, and she knew there was something about his past he was yet to reveal. She did not want to push him, though, even as she felt curious to know the answers to her questions.

"It never quite got there," he replied, gazing down at the ground.

"Things don't always turn out the way we imagine them to, I suppose. Look at me. I wasn't supposed to end up like this," Naomi said, sighing and shaking her head.

She felt she could trust Simeon, and that she could be open with him about her feelings. She liked to talk about David, but her sister and brother-in-law had heard it a thousand times. She wanted to keep his memory alive, and the best way she knew to do that was by talking about him.

"You've done a wonderful job with Hannah. She's perfect," Simeon said, and Naomi smiled.

"She's my world. I don't know what I'd do without her," Naomi admitted.

Had it not been for Hannah, Naomi knew her life would truly have ended in the aftermath of the fire. It was Hannah that gave her a reason to get up each morning and face the world. Hannah was everything to her, and glancing over to the water's edge, she smiled to see the innocence of her daughter at play.

"She's lucky to have a *mamm* like you. I know how difficult it must have been for you both – after the fire, and learning to live with David's memory, rather than his presence," Simeon replied.

Naomi nodded. That was precisely how she felt. Her memories were vivid, but they were a poor substitute for having David at her side. She could still hear his voice, feel his touch, and smell the scent of freshly laundered cotton on his shirt, but it was as though there was a veil between the two of them, a distance that no amount of willing or desire could overcome. She brushed a tear from her eye, smiling weakly at Simeon, who reached out and took her by the hand.

"I'm sorry, I'm being foolish," she said, but he shook his head.

"Not at all. You're being true to yourself. It's how you feel. You loved him – you still love him. But you can't always live in the past. Believe me, I've tried it," he said, and Naomi nodded.

"You're very kind," she said, gazing into his eyes.

All of a sudden, he leaned forward and kissed her on the cheek. It was completely unexpected, but not without feeling. She gasped, unsure of how to respond.

"I... I hope you don't mind," he said, sitting back, and looking suddenly embarrassed.

But Naomi did not mind, and she shook her head, smiling at him, their hands still clasped together.

"I don't mind," she said, just as Hannah called out to them from the water's edge.

"Look, *Mamm*, I'm throwing the stones."

Naomi looked up to watch as Hannah threw a stone into the water and the ripples spread out across the surface.

"That's very good, Hannah," Simeon called back, and Hannah clapped her hands together in delight.

They passed a pleasant afternoon by the water's edge, and when they had eaten their fill of the picnic and sat a while in the sunshine, it was time to go home. Naomi felt entirely at ease in Simeon's company, and could happily have stayed by the creek long into the evening.

"Do we have to go?" Hannah asked as Simeon picked her up to carry her in his arms up the path through the woods.

"We can't keep Simeon to ourselves all day," Naomi said, glancing at Simeon, who laughed.

"I'd like to stay all day, but I've got to get to bed at some point. I'll be up when you're still fast asleep," he replied.

Naomi thought for a moment about her dream. Being fast asleep was something she longed for, but it rarely happened. She would have made a good baker herself, for she was invariably awake when others were sleeping soundly.

"When can we see you again?" Hannah asked.

"Now, Hannah, don't get grumpy. Simeon's a busy man, he might not have time to see us again soon," Naomi said, even as she hoped that was not the case.

The afternoon they had spent together had been one of the happiest she could remember, and the thought of seeing Simeon again was foremost in her mind, the memory of the kiss lingering in her thoughts.

"Oh, I've got plenty of time. Don't you worry. We'll arrange another picnic soon, or perhaps the two of you can come to the bakery and learn another recipe. Would you like that?" he asked.

Hannah nodded. "I'd like it a lot," she replied.

They had come in sight of the house now, and Simeon put Hannah down so that she could run on ahead.

"It's been a lovely afternoon," she said, turning to him and smiling.

"I've had a wonderful time. You're so..." he began, but he was interrupted by a call from the porch.

"Hannah, you come to me now," John was saying, and Naomi looked up, surprised by the tone in her brother-in-law's voice.

Naomi looked up to see Lily hurrying down the steps to sweep Hannah into her arms. Her sister looked anxious, and Naomi hurried forward, curious to know what was going on.

"What's happening?" she asked, but as she and Simeon approached the porch, another figure appeared behind John, a tall, slender woman Naomi had never seen before.

"Oh, my..." Simeon exclaimed, stopping dead in his tracks as the woman fixed him with an angry glare.

CHAPTER TEN

aomi was confused. The woman was staring angrily at Simeon, and now she pointed her finger at him.

"You didn't exactly make it easy to find you, Simeon," she said.

Simeon faltered. "I... I didn't want to be found."

"What's going on?" Naomi asked as she watched Lily hurry Hannah inside.

"Naomi, this is Penelope Stoll. Simeon's betrothed," John replied.

Naomi's eyes grew wide with disbelief as inside her heart was torn apart.

She had known there was something about Simeon, something about his past which he had been reluctant to reveal, but to learn it concerned a woman... his betrothed... that was too much to bear. Tears welled up in her eyes, and she shook her head in disbelief at her own naivety. She had allowed herself to be entirely taken in by him, and Hannah, too, had trusted him.

"Betrothed, but absent. Simeon promised to marry me back in Ohio, then ran off to New York, leaving me heartbroken. But I'm willing to give him a second chance – now that I've found him," Penelope said.

She was an attractive woman, though her face was contorted into a scowl beneath her *kapp*. Naomi stared at her in astonishment. It was as though she had made her mind up over the matter and now intended to claim what she believed was hers.

Simeon looked shocked.

"You can't just turn up here and make demands like that, Penelope. You know why I left Blessing Bridge. It was to get away from you. You were flirting with every man in town. I didn't know where I stood. You embarrassed me, and I didn't want anything more to do with you," Simeon replied, fixing Penelope with a defiant stare.

She took two paces forward, pointing her finger at him, as Naomi looked on in utter disbelief.

"You swore to marry me, Simeon. You made me a promise, and you've broken that promise," she exclaimed.

"And you made a promise to be faithful. I couldn't marry someone like you. I thought we'd left all this behind. Why don't you just leave it? I can't believe you've followed me out here. And for what? Did you really think I'd just agree to marry you and forget everything that's happened? I don't want to marry you," he exclaimed.

Penelope's face turned scarlet, and she clenched her fists with rage.

"You made a promise!" she cried, her words echoing across the yard and causing a flock of birds in a nearby tree to rise into the air in fright.

"That was before my sister died. I couldn't do it, Penelope. I couldn't pretend everything was all right. You weren't what I needed – you hardly seemed to care," he replied, shaking his head and turning away.

This was all too much for Naomi, and she stared at him in astonishment, unable to take in what was being said. It all seemed too incredible for words. Simeon had said nothing about his sister's death, nor his betrothal to this woman. Tears welled up in Naomi's eyes, and she stared at Simeon, shaking her head, as John stepped forward.

"I think you've got a lot of explaining to do, Simeon," he said.

"I know this is all a shock, but... I can explain, I promise you," Simeon said, turning to Naomi with an imploring look on his face.

But it was all too much for Naomi. She had taken a huge risk in trusting Simeon, and now it seemed that risk was proving disastrous. She thought of David, of his kind, smiling face, and what he would think if he knew she was mixed up in such a scandalous mess. She glanced at Penelope, whose face remained like thunder, and back to Simeon, who was staring at her with wide, imploring eyes.

"I don't want to hear it," she said, turning away from him.

"Please, Naomi, let me explain. It's not what you think," Simeon replied, but Naomi had heard enough.

"I need to find Hannah, I need to focus on my family," she said, and not waiting for his reply, she fled up the steps and into the house.

CHAPTER ELEVEN

Simeon was left standing on the path, staring after Naomi. He could not believe the audacity of Penelope in coming to Faith's Creek to confront him in such a manner. He had only just begun to believe that the past was behind him and to look forward to the future. He was about to turn to Penelope when John raised his voice.

"I thought you'd make a good match for Naomi. I thought you might help her find happiness again," he said, shaking his head.

"And that's what I want. I like her. I think she's wonderful," Simeon exclaimed, even as Penelope tutted.

"You can't think like that. It's not fair to me," she exclaimed.

"It was over between us, you knew that. I never wanted you to come here," Simeon retorted, pointing his finger at her angrily.

"Well... I don't know what to think," John said, and with a final glance at Simeon, he turned away and went back inside the house.

Simeon and Penelope were left alone, and Simeon sighed, feeling as though any progress he had made since the death of his sister now lay in ruins.

Belinda's death had hit him hard, and by leaving Blessing Bridge, Simeon had hoped to make a fresh start. He had gone to New York in the hope of disappearing, his break with Penelope having been anything but cordial. She was a woman of loose morals, and there was not a man in Blessing Bridge who had not been on the receiving end of her charms. But none of that had seemed to matter, and in her own bizarre manner, Penelope still believed that a betrothal once promised still bound them together.

"I don't have anything to say to you," he said, turning to walk off down the path.

"And that's it, is it? I come all this way to find you and you think I'll just walk away?" she replied, hurrying to catch up with him.

"Did I ask you to come here? I never wanted to see you again, Penelope," Simeon said, turning to her and scowling.

"Won't you come back home? My life hasn't been the same without you," she exclaimed, taking hold of his arm.

Simeon remembered this tactic well enough. Penelope could switch personas in an instant. He had no doubt she had played the role of a jilted bride to perfection when she had arrived at the home of the Lengacher's, and now she would try to manipulate him, too. It had worked before – he had taken her back on numerous occasions – but it would not work again.

"Neither's mine. It's been better," he said, shaking off her hand and striding off towards the gate.

"How can you say that? How can you be so cruel?" she exclaimed.

"It comes quite easily when I'm treated like this," he replied.

Penelope had ruined any chance he might have had with Naomi, be it as a friend, or something more. He had always intended to tell her the truth about his past. But speaking about Belinda was difficult, even as he knew Naomi shared the same burden of pain as him.

"Now you're just being cruel," she exclaimed, still hurrying after him, even as he tried to get away.

"Look – I didn't ask you to come here. I don't want you here. I just want to be left alone. I've got bread to bake," he said, brushing her away.

"You can't do this to me. I won't let you," she called out, but Simeon had heard enough.

He wanted nothing more to do with her, and he would be glad if he never saw her again. But as he hurried towards the bakery, Simeon's heart was heavy with sorrow, and the thought that he might have lost Naomi forever made the world a darker place.

"How can I make her understand?" he wondered, knowing that his only chance of happiness rested on winning her back.

CHAPTER TWELVE

Over the following days, Naomi sank into a deep depression. There was no doubt in her mind that she had begun to fall in love with Simeon, and once again, the feelings of guilt resurfaced. She felt like a fool to have been so easily led into the realms of love and attachment, caught up as she had been in the fantasy of a man who had seemed the perfect gentleman. But looks could be deceptive, and she was annoyed with herself for so easily falling under his charms.

"You weren't to know," she kept telling herself, even as she wondered, too, if she had been too hasty in running away.

She had not heard the full story – the death of Simeon's sister, the truth about Penelope, the reasons for Simeon moving from Blessing Bridge to New York. There were so many unanswered questions, questions which Naomi knew needed answering if she was ever to find peace once again. Penelope had remained in Faith's Creek, and her presence seemed like a challenge. Naomi wondered if she blamed her for trying to steal her man, and the thought made her wary and uncomfortable at the prospect of leaving the house. Instead, she remained at home, brooding and trying to work out a way forward.

"You can't stay inside forever, Naomi," Lily said, as the two sisters sat by the stove.

John was out, and Hannah was sitting quietly at the table drawing a picture.

"I can try," Naomi replied.

"You said yourself, that you need to know the truth. Perhaps it's time to talk to him. The two of you were just starting to know one another," Lily said.

"And look where that got me. I'm through with getting to know anyone," Naomi replied, even as she did not entirely believe her own words.

She *did* want to talk to Simeon, but the thought of another confrontation like the previous one terrified her.

She did not want to encounter Penelope, nor risk discovering more unsettling truths.

"You don't mean that, you just... oh, my," Lily said, suddenly clutching at her stomach.

Naomi got to her feet and hurried to her sister's side, just as Lily gave a cry of pain.

"The *boppli*?" Naomi said, and Lily nodded.

"I think so," she replied, gasping as she spoke.

Naomi helped her to her feet, knowing she needed to get her into bed before the contractions became too much.

"What's wrong with Aunt Lily?" Hannah asked as Naomi helped her sister up the stairs.

"It's all right, Hannah. Just keep drawing," Naomi replied, supporting Lily as they reached the top step.

She got her into bed, pulling the blankets over her and trying her best to reassure her.

"I can't give birth yet. I'm not ready," Lily said.

"I don't think it works like that. You're ready when the *boppli's* ready to come. It'll be all right. I'll run and fetch Doctor Yoder. You need to keep breathing, in and out. Deep breaths, all right?" Naomi said, recalling the

·moment of Hannah's birth when Lily had said much the same to her.

Forgetting her shawl, Naomi hurried out of the house, calling out to Hannah to stay put. Doctor Yoder's house was only around half a mile from the smallholding, and Naomi took to her heels, running as fast as she could. The track ran across the cornfields and down a lane, but as she rounded a corner, Naomi came face to face with the one person she had hoped never to see again. Penelope looked equally surprised, as Naomi stopped to catch her breath.

"Running away, are you?" Penelope asked a note of disdain in her voice.

"It's my sister. She's about to give birth. I need to find Doctor Yoder," Naomi replied, not willing to rise to Penelope's condescending tone.

"You mean the one who lives across the way there? I just saw him going out in his buggy. You won't catch him now," Penelope said with a sneer.

Naomi stared at her in horror. "But she's about to give birth. I need someone who knows what to do," she replied, and Penelope narrowed her eyes.

"Simeon knows all about birth," she said.

Naomi gave an exasperated cry.

This was not the time to play games or score points. Her sister's life was at risk, and Naomi was not about to get into an argument over matrimonial matters.

"It's not Simeon I'm interested in, it's my sister, she's..." Naomi began, but Penelope interrupted her.

"I'll get help. You get back to her," she said, and there was such a change in the tone of her voice that Naomi could not help but believe in the sincerity of her words.

"You'll do that?" Naomi replied.

Penelope nodded. "Go back to your sister. She can't be on her own," she said.

Naiomi turned on her heels and ran back towards the house, not knowing what to make of this seemingly altruistic gesture on Penelope's part. When she arrived, she found Hannah still drawing at the dining table, and she rushed upstairs, where Lily's contractions had now begun.

"Did you find Doctor Yoder?" she gasped, as Naomi took her hand in hers.

"Not exactly... he's coming, though," she said, expecting Penelope to have gone in search of the doctor, whom she had seen leaving his house a short while before.

But as she had told her sister, there was no time like the present, and when a *boppli* was to be born, it would not wait for a doctor or a midwife. It would arrive precisely when it wanted to, and this *boppli* was impatient. Naomi helped her sister into a more comfortable position before bringing more towels and a kettle of boiled water from downstairs. As she was carrying it upstairs, the door opened, and to her relief, John appeared, whistling in complete oblivion to the scene unfolding upstairs.

"Are you making coffee upstairs now?" he asked, smiling bemusedly at Naomi,

She let out a sigh of relief. "Thank goodness you're here. It's Lily, she's gone into labor," she said.

John's eyes grew wide with astonishment.

He did not even pause to pull off his boots, and instead, he clattered up the stairs after Naomi, bursting into the bedroom and rushing to Lily's side.

"I'm so sorry. I didn't know. You were fine when I left this morning. Has someone run for the doctor?" he exclaimed.

"He's coming, don't worry. But I don't think we've got time to wait," she said, as Lily winced in pain at a further shuddering contraction.

There was to be no waiting, and with John holding one hand, and Naomi holding the other, Lily went into labor. Naomi did her best, coaxing her sister to push and breathe. Lily screamed in pain, even as Naomi tried to reassure her, and when the *boppli* was finally born, she lay back on the bed, exhausted and breathless.

"It's over, Lily, you did so well," John said, putting his arms around her.

Naomi cut the umbilical cord, scooping the infant up into her arms and patting him – for it was a boy – on the back.

"Is it all right?" Lily asked, but Naomi was worried.

The *boppli* was not breathing. She patted him on the back again, gently, at first, and then harder.

"Come on little one, take a deep breath," she said, the panic rising inside her at the thought of what might happen – of what was happening.

"Is something wrong?" John asked, rising to his feet.

"It's just... he's not breathing," Naomi said.

Lily gave a cry of anguish.

"No... my *boppli*... he can't be. Don't say it, Naomi!"

"It'll be all right. He just needs to take a breath, that's all," Naomi said, even as she felt entirely helpless in the face of such an awful situation.

At that moment, footsteps could be heard on the stairs, and Naomi breathed a sigh of relief, expecting Doctor Yoder to walk through the door. But as she turned, it was not Doctor Yoder who appeared, but Simeon, followed by Penelope.

"What's he doing here?" John said raising his arms in the air.

Simeon glanced at the *boppli* in Naomi's arms and seemed to know at once what to do. He took the newborn infant in his arms, ignoring John's protests, and now he held him, pushing his little finger gently into the baby's mouth.

"What's happening? What's wrong with him?" Lily asked, struggling to sit up in bed, even as Naomi bid her be still.

"It's all right, he's clearing the airways," she said, recognizing what Simeon was attempting to do.

With a sudden choking sound, the *boppli* spluttered into life and began to cry, his screams filling the room. Naomi let out a sigh of relief, and Simeon glanced at her, smiling nervously.

"He just needed a bit of help, that's all," he said, handing the *boppli* to Naomi and taking a step back.

Naomi gazed down at the infant, who was now very much alive. Tears welled up in her eyes, and she gave thanks to *Gott* for delivering them from what had been so close to a disaster.

"Oh, thank you, oh, I can't..." Lily began, as Naomi placed the little boy in her arms.

"It's all right. Just stay calm. He's all right," she said, putting the back of her hand on her sister's cheek.

It felt warm to the touch, and Naomi knew how close they had all come to disaster. Doctor Yoder would still need to be summoned. But in the meantime, the family could simply enjoy the happy arrival of the newborn, a true gift from *Gott*.

"I'm grateful to you, Simeon," John said, holding his hand out in an act of reconciliation.

"I'm just glad I was here to help, that's all. He'll be all right," Simeon replied.

Naomi watched as Simeon took a step back. Penelope had remained quiet the whole time, but now she made a move to leave the room.

"Thank you," Naomi called out, but Penelope was gone, and Simeon followed.

Naomi felt torn. She wanted to remain at her sister's side, whilst she was also desperate to thank Simeon again for his kindness. The thought of coming so close to losing the *boppli* filled her with horror. Their family had already endured so much, and they owed Simeon everything.

"Don't be a stranger," John called out, but Simeon was gone.

"I'm exhausted," Lily said.

Naomi kneeled at her side. "Don't worry, I'll stay here with you. I'll make sure the *boppli's* all right. Get some rest."

Lily closed her eyes.

But despite her promise to keep vigil, Naomi felt torn between her sister and Simeon. There was no doubt in her mind as to what they owed him, and Naomi wondered what she might do to reconnect with him and show her gratitude. He had saved the *boppli's* life. Without his intervention, they would surely have been forced to endure another tragic loss.

"We owe him so much," she said to herself, willing to put the events of the past few days behind them, if only Simeon was willing, too.

CHAPTER THIRTEEN

*N*aomi stayed at Lily's side throughout the rest of the day and through the night. Doctor Yoder paid a call late in the evening, but having checked the newborn over thoroughly, he was pleased to pronounce him a healthy *boppli*.

"Sometimes they just need a little help to get started. But knowing what to do to help... that's another matter. You say the new baker helped?" Doctor Yoder asked.

"He knew just what to do. He put his little finger in the *boppli's* mouth to help clear the airway," Naomi replied.

Doctor Yoder nodded. "That's just what I'd have done. He's been very lucky. Have you a name?"

Lily and John had decided to name their baby Abram. Abram was the name of Naomi and Lily's *grossdaddi*, and it had been a traditional name in John's family, too.

Naomi liked the name and it made her feel the love and importance of family.

The night passed by peacefully, and when Naomi awoke the next morning – for she had fallen asleep in the chair next to her sister – she found Abram awake in the crib next to the bed, wriggling and blowing bubbles.

"He's so beautiful, Lily," she said, handing Abram to her sister.

"He looks so like John. I never used to believe that *kinner* looked like their parents, but there's no doubting he does." Lily had a smile of pure joy on her face.

At that moment, the door to the bedroom opened, and John appeared, followed by Hannah, who stared wide-eyed at the scene before her.

"Can I see him?" she asked, and Naomi nodded.

"Come in, but don't make too much noise. Just be gentle with him," she said, as Hannah came rushing to the bedside.

Naomi smiled at the sight of Hannah's look of fascination. She stared down at Abram, who was now lying in Lily's arms.

"Is he my cousin?" she asked, and Naomi nodded.

"That's right, and you've got to take good care of him, all right?" she said.

Hannah seemed to take such responsibility very seriously, and she nodded, reaching out to touch the *boppli's* tiny hand with the end of her finger.

"I will," she replied, putting her head onto one side and smiling as Abram opened his eyes.

There was a great deal to do that morning. The arrival of Abram had caught them by surprise, and Lily and John were yet to do the necessary shopping – they had no diapers, only a few clothes.

Naomi volunteered to run to the store and buy what was needed. But her motive was an ulterior one, for she also wanted to call at the bakery to see Simeon. She had been thinking about doing so all night. She wanted to thank him, and try to heal the divide between them. They had been on the edge of something special, and it pained her to think of just how easily a wedge had been driven between them.

Naomi wanted to hear his side of the story, and to see if they could put the past behind them – both his and hers.

A sweet smell was coming from the bakery as Naomi approached. In the window, all manner of cakes and loaves were on display. It was a feast for the senses, and Naomi pressed her face to the window, suddenly realizing she had not eaten since the afternoon before. But before she could think anymore about her stomach, she saw Simeon behind the counter, and taking a deep breath, she stepped through the door. He looked up at her in surprise, a nervous expression coming over his face.

"Is the *boppli* all right?" he asked.

Naomi nodded. "He's fine. Doctor Yoder came to see him. He's a healthy little boy. They've named him Abram after our *grossdaddi*," she said.

Simeon smiled. "That's a nice name, strong. I'm just glad I was able to help," he said.

Naomi closed the bakery door behind her. "You did more than help. You saved his life. If it wasn't for you, he'd have died," she said, thinking Simeon did not realize the enormity of what he had done.

"Well... I just... I did what had to be done," he said.

Naomi shook her head. In her eyes, Simeon was a hero, and the whole family owed him a great debt, one that could never be repaid.

"But how did you know what to do?" she asked, still curious as to why Penelope had summoned Simeon, instead of trying to find Doctor Yoder.

Simeon looked suddenly sad and he shook his head, sitting down on a stool behind the counter.

"Well, I... I'm sorry I wasn't honest with you about my sister, Belinda."

Naomi felt her heart stutter, were there more lies?

CHAPTER FOURTEEN

*L*ooking at Simeon she knew that she had to trust him. Tragedy happened and that didn't make it anyone's fault. This time she would listen and hear his side.

"Penelope was just stirring up trouble by coming here," Simeon said. "What we had ended a long time ago. Belinda, my sister, died in a buggy accident, but she was pregnant at the time. There was a storm, and we were caught in it on the road. The buggy flipped. Somehow, I got out unscathed, but Belinda was injured and the *boppli* came before help could come. I tried my best, but... my best wasn't good enough. I tried to save them both, but I couldn't save either of them. I've never regretted anything more than that. I thought I could run away from it, but the past has a nasty habit of catching up with you. I'm sorry I didn't tell you the truth," he said, looking up at Naomi, who had tears in her eyes.

The tragic story of his sister's death was too awful to comprehend. She understood now why he had not wanted to talk about it. He was carrying a terrible burden, one which would surely haunt him for the rest of his life. Naomi could only feel sorry for him, and she shook her head and reached out across the counter to take him by the hand.

"How awful for you," she said, fighting back the tears.

"Seeing Abram yesterday... well, I knew I had to help. I had to do something," he said.

Naomi smiled. "You certainly did that. We... I can't thank you enough."

She wanted him to understand how grateful she was. He had saved her nephew's life, and now, in full possession of the facts, she understood why he had been so unwilling to share the tragedy of his past with her. Like herself, he, too, had experienced the trauma of losing someone he loved – two people he loved – and her heart went out to him, and she wanted only to help him.

"You don't need to thank me. I did it because it was the right thing to do. I'm only glad Penelope came to find me. She's not always as bad as she seems," he said, giving Naomi a weak smile.

"But all that stuff about the two of you being betrothed and her coming here to bring you back to Ohio. Is it true?" Naomi asked.

A part of her was still holding back. She had been hurt by Penelope's revelations, and she wanted to be certain that what Simeon was telling her was true. He looked at her and sighed.

"She's got a good side and a bad side. But I think she only came here to cause trouble, and right at the moment, I was at my happiest – with you and Hannah. I might have wanted to marry her once, but not now. We broke it off a long time ago but she couldn't accept that. I wish she'd just pack her bags and leave," Simeon said, shaking his head.

A tear rolled down his cheek, and Naomi squeezed his hand across the counter. There was no doubt in her mind he was telling the truth.

"I'm sure she'll get the message eventually," she said.

Simeon nodded. "I tried to tell her. I tried to make her see sense, but then... I don't know where we stand, either. You and me, I mean," he said, fixing Naomi with a sorrowful gaze.

Naomi's heart skipped a beat. This was the moment of choice. She thought of David and of what he would say to her now. She knew he would want her to be happy, and she searched her heart, asking herself what might be if she gave in to the feelings growing there.

Simeon had proved himself a good man, a man of honesty and integrity. She wanted him in her life, and she knew Hannah did, too. She smiled at him, taking a deep breath.

"I'm sorry I got upset the other day. I didn't know the full story, and Penelope turning up like that just... well, it was too much. But I know the truth now. I know what happened, and I understand. We've only just started getting to know one another, but I want to keep getting to know you. I've come to care for you, and so has Hannah," she said.

"I don't always feel worthy of a second chance. What happened with Belinda... it hurt me so much," he said.

Naomi loosed her hand from his and made her way around to the other side of the counter. She was not sure what compelled her to do it, but she put her arms around him, wanting him to understand there was nothing that needed forgiveness. This was not about a second chance, it was about picking up where they had left off, and realizing that they both deserved to be happy.

"I haven't really smiled over the past three years. I've felt like a shadow of my old self. The only thing worth getting up for each morning was Hannah. If it weren't for her, I don't know what I'd have done. But you made me smile, and laugh, and feel happy. You made me forget what had been and think about what might have been. I was rude to you at first, but that feels like a lifetime ago. It's me that should be sorry. I didn't trust you, and when Penelope arrived on the scene, I thought you'd deceived me. But I was wrong, and I admit that. It's me who needs a second chance, or if you'd rather, we both do," she said.

Naomi was willing to put the past behind them. She wanted to move on and look to the future – a future for them both. Simeon stared at her. It was as though he had already steeled himself for rejection, and now his eyes grew wide as though in disbelief.

"You don't need to apologize. It's me that made a mistake," he said, but Naomi shook her head.

"Maybe we both did. But it doesn't matter now, none of it matters. What I mean is... I'd like to try again, if you're willing, that is," she said.

She had said it now. There was no turning back. She had made herself vulnerable to rejection. It was his decision now, and she held her breath as he fell silent. The wait seemed like an eternity, and he averted his gaze, staring at a spot behind her. Had she said the wrong thing? Naomi's heart was beating fast, and her hands were trembling, even as he took a deep breath, looking up at her and nodding.

"I'm sorry about what happened – with Penelope, I mean. She should never have come here. But perhaps the two of us can start over again – if you're willing to, that is," he said.

"I'd like that," she said, and he put his arms around her and kissed her.

"You don't know how happy I am to hear you say that," he said.

Naomi let out the breath she had been holding, it felt as if a burden was lifted from her shoulders.

"As happy as I feel," she said, laughing as the two of them joined hands.

"Why don't we go and see your nephew? We've got some good news to share," he said, and hand in hand, they left the bakery, walking happily together in the joy of a new and happy beginning.

CHAPTER FIFTEEN

Simeon could not have felt happier to be reconciled with Naomi. He had thought her lost, and that his foolish actions – the actions of the past – had caused him undue suffering in the present. But to be given a second chance – for he believed it *was* a second chance – made him feel happier than he could possibly put into words.

The two of them had visited Lily and John, and Naomi's sister and brother-in-law had been surprised to witness the reconciliation that had taken place. It was obvious to everyone that Simeon and Naomi intended to make a go of their fledgling relationship, but a thorn still remained in their side, the thorn of Penelope and what she would do next.

Penelope was renting a room close to the bakery, and she had made it her business to come each morning and speak with Simeon. There was something distasteful about her constant pleading. She wanted Simeon to take her back, and she had all manner of reasons which she used to try and persuade him. She was only doing herself a disservice, and it seemed to Simeon that she would only grow more unhappy the more he put her off.

With he and Naomi now looking to the future, Simeon knew it was time to confront his past once and for all. It was the day after he had visited *boppli* Abram with Naomi, and he had just finished taking out the freshly baked loaves from the oven to sell that day. It was still early, not even eight o'clock, when Penelope appeared at the door of the bakery and steeling himself, Simeon went to let her in.

"Simeon, I've been thinking. We could stay here, in Faith's Creek. You can't run this bakery all by yourself. I could help you. I know a little about baking, and you could teach me. What do you say?" Penelope asked, stepping over the threshold before Simeon could even invite her in.

"Look, Penelope. We need to talk," Simeon said.

In the past, he had not always been as firm with Penelope as he should have been. She had a way of worming her way through a conversation to arrive at precisely the point she wanted. Riding roughshod over everyone else's feelings. But this time, Simeon was determined not to allow her to get the upper hand.

"We are talking. We talk every day. Now, I was thinking, if I work at the counter, you can concentrate on baking. You can't do both, and..." she began, but Simeon interrupted her.

"It's not going to work, Penelope," he said.

"You mean you'd rather I worked in the kitchen and you worked at the counter? That could work. You'd have to show me how to bake, though. Do you remember when I burned that apple pie?" she said, laughing, even as she pretended not to understand what he was saying.

"I mean you being here, Penelope. It's not going to work. You can't just turn up here and expect me to agree to your demands. It's over between us. It's been over since the moment that we broke it off, since the moment I got on that Greyhound bus and set off for New York. We can't change the past, and we can't pretend as though nothing ever happened," he said, fixing her with a stern look.

Penelope was fighting back the tears, and she stammered, shaking her head as though she refused to believe what he was saying.

"You don't mean that. You just need some time to think about it. You can't waste your life here in a bakery," she exclaimed, her tone suddenly changing and a sneer coming over her face.

"A moment ago, you were all set to stay here," he replied.

Penelope laughed. "It wasn't the place I was interested in. It's you, Simeon. It's you I want. It's you I came here for. Don't you see that?" she snapped.

"I know why you came. But all you've done is cause trouble. Can't you see we'd both be happier going our separate ways? I'm staying here, and I don't want you to waste your life chasing after me when it's just not going to happen," he said, folding his arms and staring at her defiantly.

Penelope stared at him in disbelief. It seemed she had been so caught up in the fantasy of returning with him to Blessing Bridge, that she could not see beyond the possibility to anything else. Her lip was trembling, and for a moment, Simeon felt sorry for her.

"It's her, isn't it? The widow from the smallholding. It's her that's done it, isn't it?" she exclaimed.

Simeon sighed.

He had not wanted to cause an argument – though he had known it was inevitable – and he had not wanted to bring Naomi and Hannah into it, either. But the truth was simple enough. He wanted to be with Naomi and leave the past where it belonged.

"She hasn't done anything. But our feelings had changed a long while ago. We ended our relationship, you ended it as much as I. I don't want to marry you, Penelope," he said, firmly resolved to stand his ground.

She stared at him, shaking her head as though unable to believe what she was hearing.

"You'll regret it. You'll soon see what she's really like. You'll get bored of her. Well... don't expect me to wait for you. I came here thinking we had a future together, Simeon. But you've led me a merry dance," she said.

Simeon rolled his eyes. "I've been clear with you from the beginning. I didn't ask you to come here, and I'd much rather you just leave. Let's draw a line under the past," he said.

Penelope turned on her heels and marched out of the bakery. "I hope you're happy," she exclaimed, banging the door behind her.

Simeon breathed a sigh of relief. He turned to the kitchen, just as Naomi peered cautiously through. She had been listening the whole time.

"Well, that was certainly explosive," he said, as she came out and put her arms around him.

"It's done now. I think she got the message. I feel sorry for her. She just didn't seem to understand," Naomi said.

Simeon had wanted her there so she could hear exactly what was being said. He did not want Naomi to think he still had any feelings for Penelope – save pity. He had not wanted to hurt her, but he had had no other choice but to be brutally honest with her. It was the only way they could get rid of her and look to build a future together.

"I'm sorry for what she said about you," Simeon said.

Naomi only shook her head and laughed. "It's water off a duck's back. I'd probably have said the same kind of thing if I was as upset as her. Let's just forget it. She's gone now, and that's all that matters. I just hope she'll be happy, that's all," Naomi said, slipping her hand into Simeon's and squeezing it.

He felt relieved at having finally rid himself of Penelope. He had loved her once, but she had shown her true colors once too often. All Simeon wanted was a future with Naomi, a future he could now look to with hope.

"I love you," he said. "I want you to know everything about me. I left the Amish to escape Penelope but I never really left in my heart. When I came back it felt right but I never thought I could love again. I didn't think I deserved it. When I saw you I knew there was a chance for a new love for me, here in Faith's Creek. I felt healed and I wanted so much to heal you."

"I felt the same," she said. "This is my new chance to love, it doesn't replace my old love but it is time to move on, time to live again."

"You're sure about all this? I want you to be happy, too. So much has happened, so much has changed..." he began.

Naomi stopped him with a finger on his lips.

"I know I'm sure. You've proved yourself to me, and to Hannah – to us all. It's not just about Abram. I couldn't ever doubt you again, Simeon. Hannah adores you. My sister thinks you're wonderful. You and John are the firmest of friends again. And I've finally realized that David would want me to be happy. He wouldn't want me to spend the rest of my life as a grieving widow. What sort of future is that? It's no future at all, that's what it is," she replied.

Simeon breathed a sigh of relief. He could not have felt happier than he did at that moment. He had come so close to losing her, but now the future lay ahead, full of happy possibilities. He wanted only one thing: to be part of a family, and with Naomi, that possibility was his.

"I'm not trying to replace him, and I wouldn't ever let Hannah forget him," he said, and Naomi smiled.

"I'll never forget him, and I'll never stop loving him, or telling Hannah what a wonderful *daed* she had – she has. But I know he'd want me to learn to live again, and that's what I want, too," she said, smiling at Simeon, who put his arms around her and kissed her on the forehead.

"You're one in a million, Naomi. You're the only person who really understands me," he said.

"We understand one another. We know what it's like to lose the person we care about more than anything else in the world. But now we each know what it's like to find someone to build a future with, too," she said.

He looked down at her and nodded, knowing he wanted only to spend the rest of his life with her. There was still so much to discover about her, so much to learn, but Simeon knew he had found the woman with whom he would be happy forever. As he held her in his arms, he pictured their wedding day, a little house in Faith's Creek, *kinner*, and all that lay ahead of them.

"That's a future I want to share," he said, kissing her on the forehead once again and holding her close.

EPILOGUE

It was two years later, and Naomi was watching through the kitchen window as her nephew, Abram, was running across the garden with Hannah. John was outside, too, and he scooped the two *kinner* up into his arms, raising them high into the air and spinning them around, all of them laughing as they rolled onto the grass.

It was a beautiful day. The sun was high in the sky, and Naomi, Simeon, Hannah, and their new *boppli* daughter, Belinda, had come to visit Lily, John, and Abram. They lived only a few moments' walk away, and would often visit one another, happy to at last be two families, each as happy as the other.

"I can't believe how big Abram's grown. And he looks so like John, it's quite remarkable," Naomi said, turning back to Lily, who was sitting at the table drinking coffee.

They had enjoyed a delicious lunch together – fried chicken and then shoofly pie, apple fritters, cinnamon buns, and a large fruit cake, all of which had been demolished by both children and grown-ups alike. After that, they spent the afternoon just being family. The day was drawing on and soon they would eat again. Naomi felt blessed to have such a life and she thanked *Gott* for all His blessings.

"He's going to grow up to be just as tall. If not taller. I'm certain of it," Lily said, laughing and shaking her head.

Naomi came to join her at the table, taking up an embroidery frame she was working on. She was embroidering Belinda's name and her dates above a small picture of a teddy bear. Belinda was named after Simeon's sister, and her arrival had made the family complete. She was a sweet little thing, always smiling and happy. Hannah adored being an older sister to her, and she had been a great help to Naomi in the past months since the *boppli's* arrival.

Naomi and Simeon had married some eighteen months previously, in a ceremony presided over by Bishop

Beiler. The cakes had been spectacular and had been made by Simeon himself to celebrate the special day. They still had a piece of one, kept for posterity, and when Belinda had been born, they had eaten a small piece by way of celebration.

"Hannah looks just like David. It's something in her eyes. Whenever I look at her, I'm reminded of him," Naomi said.

Lily reached out and put her hand on Naomi's and smiled. "He'll always be here, and in here," she said, pointing to Naomi's heart.

Naomi nodded. She knew she would never forget David, and whilst life had changed for them all, his memory would remain. She had learned she could love again, and that doing so was no dishonor to her husband's memory, but rather a recognition that she, too, had a life to live, and a responsibility to do what was right by way of Hannah, too.

"I don't have that dream anymore. The one I always used to. I can think about him without getting upset and teary. It's nice to have those memories," she said.

Lily nodded. "It's *Gott's* blessing on you. You've been through so much. You deserve the happiness you've found," she said.

Naomi smiled.

A loaf of honey bread was in the oven, and the timer now went off, so that Lily sprang to her feet, just as John, Abram, and Hannah came in from the garden. They were in high spirits, and Abram came running over to Naomi, tugging at her skirts with an excited look on his face.

"Can I see the *boppli?*" he asked, for Abram – like Hannah – was fascinated by the newborn.

They were like siblings, and Naomi smiled, rising to her feet and lifting the little boy into her arms.

"Let's go together, and Hannah can come, too. She might be sleeping though. Let's go and find Simeon and see," she said, beckoning Hannah to come, too.

Simeon was in Lily's and John's bedroom. It was the only quiet room in the house. As they entered, he turned to them and raised his finger to his lips.

"She's fast asleep," he whispered, as Abram strained to catch a glimpse of the *boppli* in the crib which had once been his.

"She's always asleep," he whispered, sounding somewhat disappointed.

"You played with her this morning," Naomi said, smiling at Abram, who nodded.

"When she can stay up longer, we'll play all day, won't we?" he said, and Naomi laughed.

"I'm sure you will. Now, why don't you and Hannah go and help your *mamm* lay the table," Naomi said, fearful that Belinda would wake up at any moment.

She set Abram down and sent the two of them off downstairs, before joining Simeon next to the crib. He put his arm around her, and the two of them looked down at the sleeping *boppli*. She was perfect, and Naomi thanked *Gott* for the gift of not one, but two, perfect little girls.

"She went right off. She must have been tired," Simeon said, as Naomi rested her head on his shoulder.

"We'll let her sleep whilst we have dinner, then we'd better get her home, don't you think?" she said, and Simeon nodded.

"But not until I've had a slice of your sister's apple pie. It's so nice to have a family dinner together, don't you think?" he replied.

Naomi agreed. She was so pleased that at last, she could be a sister to Lily, rather than a lodger. She enjoyed inviting Lily, John, and Abram to her and Simeon's home for dinner, and sharing special times of the year together. They were a family, and at last, Naomi felt she contributed her fair share to that family, rather than using the others as her crutch and support. There was no doubt her relationship with Lily had greatly improved since her marriage to Simeon. They were not only sisters but best friends, too.

"I do. We're a real family again. It's priceless," she said, just as footsteps could be heard on the stairs.

"*Mamm*, Simeon, look at what I did," Hannah exclaimed, bursting into the room and clearly forgetting Belinda was fast asleep.

"Don't wake the *boppli*, Hannah," Naomi exclaimed, trying to keep her voice to a whisper.

Hannah held up a picture for her to see, one which caused her heart to melt.

The picture showed Naomi, Simeon, Hannah, and *boppli* Belinda. They were standing in a beautiful garden and the sun was shining down on them. A single cloud was in the sky, and on it, another figure sat with a broad smile on his face. There was no doubt it was David, and Naomi felt the tears well up in her eyes.

"That's beautiful, Hannah," Naomi said, and she stooped down and put her arms around her daughter.

Simeon did the same, and for a moment, the three of them were silent. Naomi gave thanks to *Gott* for this wonderful blessing. They were a family, and she knew they would forever honor David's memory whilst living their lives to the fullest.

"What a wonderful picture, Hannah. I think we should put it up when we get home," Simeon said.

Hannah nodded. "I drew *Daed*, too," she said.

Naomi nodded, brushing the tears from her eyes as Simeon put his arm around her and kissed her.

"We'll always remember *Daed*, won't we?" she said.

Just then, Belinda stirred, and Naomi turned and lifted her out of the crib and shushed her. She opened her eyes and began to wriggle.

"I think someone's hungry," Simeon said.

Naomi laughed. "Do you mean you or her? Dinner does smell good. We'd better go down," she said, but Simeon caught her arm and smiled at her.

"We're blessed, aren't we? All of us. You, me, Lily, John, Hannah, Belinda, and Abram. It's taken some heartache to get here, but we have," he said, and Naomi nodded.

"I'd never have gotten here if it weren't for you," she said, and Simeon leaned forward and kissed her.

"Nor I without you. Love is like sunshine after the rain," he said, just as Hannah tugged at Naomi's dress.

"I'm hungry," she said, and Naomi smiled.

"Then we'd better go and eat. I think there's a loaf of honey bread to go with that apple pie," she replied, and together they made their way downstairs as a family, the family which now brought Naomi the happiness she had thought lost, the happiness which had so unexpectedly found her.

LOVE, HEART AND FAMILY 30 BOOK INSPIRATIONAL BOX SET - PREVIEW

A dozen pies were cooling on the windowsill, Katy Zook had just removed three more from the oven, their sweet aroma filling the kitchen with the scent of apples and cinnamon. She looked down and smiled, for baking brought her pleasure. The pies were her pride and she was always proud of how wonderful they looked.

As they sat there all tempting, the thought of cutting into them was too much to resist. Placing two on the cooling rack, she set the other down on her workbench, taking a knife she cut it open. The aroma filled the air with apples making her stomach rumble. The filling still bubbled with heat, as she placed a slice into a dish and covered it with heavy cream.

She was just about to take a spoon from the drawer and begin to eat when a knock at the door caused her to startle. Katy was used to being alone, living in the house which had belonged to her parents for fifty years and which her grandfather had built when first they had come to join the community at Faith's Creek. When her parents died, Katy had been left alone. She made a simple living by selling the pies and pastries she was famous for, along with eggs from the chickens she kept out back.

"It's just me," came the familiar voice of her friend Susan Schrock.

Katy set down her spoon with a sigh and went to answer the door.

Susan was her usual maternal self, looking radiant and even more pregnant than the last time Katy had seen her. Susan's stomach was bulging under the plain blue dress she wore, her hair tied up and tucked beneath her *kapp*. She was carrying Rosella, her first child, in her arms and bustled inside, without waiting to be invited.

"I was just..." Katy began, and Susan raised her eyebrow.

"Eating your profits?" she asked.

Katy smiled. "Won't you sit down? I'll make some *kaffe*. Will you have a slice of pie? It's already cut," Katy said.

Susan laughed. "They smell delicious. I don't think there's a better baker than you in the whole county. Those chocolate walnut buns you made last week were delicious. Bishop Beiler couldn't stop talking about them when I saw him earlier," she said, setting Rosella down on the rug and taking a seat at the table.

"Amos Beiler is one of my best customers, he's asked for an apple turnover for next week. It's Sarah's birthday and he wants to do something special for her," Katy said, setting a kettle of water on the burner to boil.

"Samuel's like that too, he does such lovely things for me. Do you know, the other day he went out and picked me flowers from the meadow by the creek and had them in a vase waiting for me when I got home. It was the sweetest thing, I'm so lucky," Susan said, as Katy cut her a slice of pie.

The two women had been friends for many years, but their lives had taken something of a different course. While Susan was married and content with a healthy, happy child and another on the way, Katy had found little solace in the hope of marriage. Her courting year resulting in nothing but the heartache of seeing herself passed over, always ignored and rejected.

"Cream?" she asked.

Susan nodded. "It looks divine. It seems like we came at just the right moment," she said, taking the spoon which Katy offered and digging in hungrily.

"How's Rosella doing? Does she realize she's about to have a baby brother?" Katy asked.

"Or sister, I don't know what it is. I know you can find out, but I just don't think that's right. Why not let it be a surprise as *Gott* intended?" Susan said, taking another spoonful of the pie.

"A girl then a boy, isn't that what you want?" Katy asked.

Susan shrugged her shoulders. "So long as they grow up happy, healthy, and faithful I'll settle for anything," she replied, "this is good pie."

"That's the one thing I'm good at, I suppose," Katy said.

Susan frowned. "Now, I don't want to hear that. You're always putting yourself down, Katy. There are lots of things you're good at. Didn't your cross stitch win first prize at the craft fair last year? And they were falling over themselves to buy your goat's milk soaps, I've still got one and Samuel was just saying the other day how delightful it smelled and..." Susan said.

Katy interrupted her. "It's not that... I can bake and sew and craft and mend all you like, but what's the point if there's no one to share it all with," she said, glancing at Rosella, who was rolling and giggling on the rug by the stove.

"Oh, Katy, don't talk like that. You're twenty-two, hardly an old maid," Susan replied, leaning over and patting Katy on the arm.

"But I'm not exactly inundated with offers either, am I?" Katy replied, looking down at her flour-covered apron and sighing.

It was not that she was unattractive, she was pretty even, but in the years of her mother's illness and with her father gone, it was food that had become her comfort. Pies, pastries, bread, cakes, sweet treats, and savory, they had all been Katy's solace and now her figure was almost as round as Susan's. Without realizing it she had become overweight. Now, she was the subject of teasing by the local children, who would call her fat and throw sweets at her as she walked by. It upset her deeply and the more she thought about it, the worse it got.

Katy had no confidence, in herself or in the opinions of others. She was plain Katy, the baker who ate too many of her own pies, hardly an object of attraction to any man. Compared to Susan, Katy felt a failure and she knew it would have upset her mother dearly to know how unhappy her daughter was. She was an only child and if it were not for the meager living she earned selling her produce to the people of Faith's Creek she would have nothing to call her own or be proud of.

"There's someone for everyone, Katy. I believe that. Don't you?" Susan said.

Katy sighed. She knew that Susan was trying to cheer her up but at that moment, she felt nothing but despair. She had thought about it a lot recently, perhaps because she had been baking for a wedding. The happy couple seemed so very much in love that it had set her thinking about her own future too. How she longed to be that bride, to have a man to call her own, a man that would be kind and decent towards her and love her for who she was.

"I'm starting to wonder," Katy replied, finishing her slice of pie, and wondering whether it would be glutinous to cut herself a second slice.

"You'll find someone, or better still, he'll find you. Besides, you've never shown any interest in all that before, you always say you don't want children. That was delicious, by the way," Susan said, laying down her spoon.

"Another slice?" Katy asked, thinking that it would not appear as bad if Susan accepted her offer.

"I couldn't possibly, but I'll take one for Samuel. He's been out working on the farm all day, he'll be glad of it. I only wish I could bake like you. My pies always over bake on the top and stay raw on the bottom," she said, shaking her head.

"That's because you put them on a cold tray. Heat your tray first, then put the pie tin on top, that way the heat of the oven goes all around," Katy said.

Susan laughed. "See, I told you you're good at things and if the way to a man's heart is through his stomach, then you'll have the whole of Faith's Creek queueing up to marry you," Susan said, reaching down to pick up Rosella, who had started to cry.

The two women passed a pleasant morning, as Katy continued baking and Susan imparted what she referred to as 'interesting information,' which otherwise might be interpreted as gossip. When the clock struck noon, she looked up and let out a cry of exclamation, clambering to her feet and putting on her shawl.

"Is it something I said?" Katy asked.

Susan laughed. "I said I'd have Samuel's dinner on the table for half-past. I'd best get going," she said, scooping up Rosella, who had once again been playing happily on the rug.

"Take a loaf of bread and the rest of the pie. He'll not want much else if you place that in front of him. You take care now and call in anytime, I'm always happy to see you," Katy said.

"Don't be a stranger now, you're always welcome with us too. I'll see you at the service on Sunday, if not before. Don't forget, it's in Rueben Petershiem's barn this week, they're having food afterward too," she said, as Katy opened the door for her.

"I know, Almina's got me baking three cakes for her," Katy said, and with that, she waved Susan off, watching, as she made her way along the track which wound its way through the cornfields towards Faith's Creek.

She closed the door and returned to the kitchen, the lingering, sweet smell of cinnamon making her hungry once again. Susan's words were playing on her mind. She had always shied away from conversations about children, owing to her own self-belief that she would never have any. But the claim that she did not want children was false, a means of deflecting the very real desire she felt, as her maternal instincts grew. Seeing Susan so happy had made her long even more for a child and the thought that she might never have one weighed heavily on her mind.

* * *

Grab all 30 books in this great value box set for FREE with Kindle Unlimited. Love, Heart, and Family 30 Book Inspirational Collection

ALSO BY SARAH MILLER

All my books are FREE on Kindle Unlimited

If you love Amish Romance, the sweet, clean stories of Sarah Miller receive free stories and join me for the latest news on upcoming books here

These are some of my reader favorites:

The Amish Landscape

The Amish Family and Faith Collection

Find all Sarah's books on Amazon and click the yellow follow button

This book is dedicated to the wonderful Amish people and the faithful life that they live.

Go in peace, my friends.

As an independent author, Sarah relies on your support. If you enjoyed this book, please leave a review on Amazon or Goodreads.

ABOUT THE AUTHOR

Sarah Miller was born in Pennsylvania and spent her childhood close to the Amish people. Weekends were spent doing chores; quilting or eventually babysitting in the community. She grew up to love their culture and the simple lifestyle and had many Amish friends. The one thing that you can guarantee when you are near the Amish, Sarah believes is that you will feel close to God.

Many years later she married Martin who is the love of her life and moved to England. There she started to write stories about the Amish. Recently after a lot of persuasion from her best friend she has decided to publish her stories. They draw on inspiration from her relationship with the Amish and with God and she hopes you enjoy reading them as much as she did writing them. Many of the stories are based on true events but names have been changed and even though they are authentic at times artistic license has been used.

Sarah likes her stories simple and to hold a message and they help bring her closer to her faith. She currently lives in Yorkshire, England with her husband Martin and seven very spoiled chickens.

She would love to meet you on Facebook at https://www.facebook.com/SarahMillerBooks

Sarah hopes her stories will both entertain and inspire and she wishes that you go with God.

Made in the USA
Coppell, TX
01 September 2022